Margaret the
Space Cabbage

D1092965

'NTY

MR BLOOM'S NURSERY: MARGARET THE SPACE CABBAGE
A BANTAM BOOK 978 0 857 51248 2

Published in Great Britain by Bantam,
an imprint of Random House Children's Publishers UK
A Random House Group Company.

This edition published 2013

1 3 5 7 9 10 8 6 4 2

Bantam Books are published by Random House Children's Publishers UK,
61–63 Uxbridge Road, London W5 5SA

www.**randomhousechildrens**.co.uk

Addresses for companies within The Random House Group Limited can be found at:
www.randomhouse.co.uk/offices.htm

THE RANDOM HOUSE GROUP Limited Reg. No. 954009

A CIP catalogue record for this book is available from the British Library

Printed in China

The Random House Group Limited supports The Forest Stewardship Council (FSC®),
the leading international forest certification organization. Our books carrying the FSC label
are printed on FSC®-certified paper. FSC is the only forest certification scheme endorsed
by the leading environmental organizations, including Greenpeace. Our paper procurement
policy can be found at www.randomhouse.co.uk/environment

Margaret the Space Cabbage

BANTAM BOOKS

Hello there, Tiddlers! How are you today? Welcome to my allotment, where there's always a lot for us to see and do!

I've been checking on the wiggly worms inside my Compostarium. They have a very important job to do in the garden! Do you know what it is? It starts with feeding them my kitchen rubbish, like old tea bags and vegetable peelings. Yuck!

The worms will eat the rubbish, and then they'll turn it into a lovely rich mixture in their tummies. When that mixture comes out it's called compost, and it's really useful because it helps my plants to grow!

Now let's go inside the nursery, where the Veggies are waiting. Then I'll tell you a story, about the time Margaret wanted to visit the moon . . .

One day, I heard Margaret counting.
"5, 4, 3, 2, 1, BLAST OFF!"
she cried.
"What are you up to, Margaret?" I
asked her.

8

"I'm zooming off to the moon!" she told me.

"Wow, what an adventure! That must mean you're the first cabbage in space, Margaret!" I said.

I really liked the idea.

"No, there's already been a cabbage in space, Mr Bloom," Raymond told me.

"Yes, it's in my magazine," Margaret said. "Raymond was reading the story to me."

"But I can't read her name. It's too
difficult," Raymond said.

"Cabb ..."

"Cabbi ..."

"Cabbid ..."

"OK, let's have a look," I said.
I took the magazine from him and
read, "*Cabb-id-gi-kova*. That's a
long name, isn't it, Veggies!"

"So, you want to be like her do you, Margaret?" I asked her.

"Oh, yes I do!" Margaret said.

"I'd like to zoom off to the moon and fly past the stars. Woosh!"

Suddenly, I had an idea . . .

"Maybe we could help you to be a

space cabbage, Margaret," I said.

"Really? Oh Mr Bloom, yes please!"

Margaret cried.

Compo's fans began to **whirr**, his pistons started to **chug** and some bubbles floated across the nursery. Compo wanted to help to make Margaret's dream come true!

With a loud **toot toot**, Compo's
drawer popped open.

Inside I found a big bottle of glue
and a large sheet of black paper.

There was also some shiny tin foil
and lots of gold star-shaped stickers!

Now I had all I needed to make a starry surprise for Margaret.
I began cutting and sticking . . .
When I'd finished, I put down my scissors and left the scraps of paper beside the empty glue bottle.

Then I pinned the sheet of black
paper onto the wall.
The tin foil and gold sticker stars
really sparkled!

"Ooh, starry bean!" said Colin, when
the Veggies saw my space scene.

How many stars can you count,
Tiddlers?

While we were busy counting the stars, the cheeky Wee MacGregors were up to something.

Ever so quietly, they began to suck up the scraps of paper. Then they took the empty glue bottle.

The Wee MacGregors were making
the rubbish into something useful,
just like those wiggly worms did!
Can you guess what it was, Tiddlers?

Using the scraps of paper, the empty glue bottle and a cardboard box, the Wee MacGregors made a space rocket for Margaret!

"Look at the rocket, Veggies!" I said.
"Ooh!" the Veggies gasped.
"That's really nice of you, Wee
MacGregors!" I told them.

I carefully placed Margaret in
the rocket.
"Now you're ready to blast off into
space!" I told her.
It's time for the countdown now,
Tiddlers. Join in!

5, 4, 3, 2, 1,
BLAST OFF!

Margaret the space cabbage zoomed into space. She flew past the stars, towards the moon . . .

So Margaret *did* get to be a cabbage in space, just like she dreamed! What do you think of that, Tiddlers?

Now it's time for me and the Veggies to say goodbye. Come and see us again soon, for another exciting adventure!

Make your own . . . space rocket

Want to turn rubbish into something really useful, just like the Wee MacGregors did? Ask a grown up to help you and then follow these simple steps!

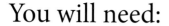

You will need:
- A cardboard box
- Scissors
- Tin foil
- Glue
- A plastic bottle
- Sticky tape

STEP 1

Ask a grown up to cut a hole in the centre of the cardboard box, so that your toy can look out.

STEP 2

Then tape the plastic bottle onto the top of the cardboard box.

STEP 3

Next, cut out lots of star shapes from the tin foil and glue them all over the cardboard box and plastic bottle.

STEP 4

Once the glue is dry, your space rocket is ready for blast off!

Don't miss these other exciting books from Mr Bloom's Nursery!